SATYAJI

THE ADVENTURES OF
FELUDA

THE
CRIMINALS OF KATHMANDU

PUFFIN BOOKS

An imprint of Penguin Random House

PUFFIN BOOKS

USA | Canada | UK | Ireland | Australia
New Zealand | India | South Africa | China

Puffin Books is part of the Penguin Random House group of companies
whose addresses can be found at global.penguinrandomhouse.com

Published by Penguin Random House India Pvt. Ltd
4th Floor, Capital Tower 1, MG Road,
Gurugram 122 002, Haryana, India

Penguin
Random House
India

First published in Puffin by Penguin Books India 2004
This edition published in Puffin Books by Penguin Random House India 2019

Copyright © The Estate of Satyajit Ray 2004
This translation copyright © Penguin Books India 2004

ISBN 9780143335726

Typeset in Garamond Book by Manipal Technologies Limited, Manipal
Printed at Repro India Limited

www.penguin.co.in

MIX
Paper from
responsible sources
FSC® C047271

PUFFIN BOOKS

THE ADVENTURES OF FELUDA
THE CRIMINALS OF KATHMANDU

Satyajit Ray (1921–92) was one of the greatest filmmakers of his time, renowned for films like *Pather Panchali*, *Charulata*, *Aranyer Din Ratri* and *Ghare Baire*. He was awarded the Academy Honorary Award for Lifetime Achievement by the Academy of Motion Picture Arts and Science in 1992, and in the same year, was also honoured with the Bharat Ratna.

Ray was also a writer of repute, and his short stories, novellas, poems and articles, written in Bengali, have been immensely popular ever since they first began to appear in the children's magazine *Sandesh* in 1961. Among his most famous creations are the master sleuth Feluda and the scientist Professor Shonku.

*

Gopa Majumdar has translated several works from Bengali to English, the most notable of these being Ashapurna Debi's *Subarnalata*, Taslima Nasrin's *My Girlhood* and Bibhutibhushan Bandyopadhyay's *Aparajito*, for which she won the Sahitya Akademi Award in 2001. She has translated several volumes of Satyajit Ray's short stories and all of the Feluda stories for Penguin Books India. She is currently translating Ray's Professor Shonku stories, which are forthcoming in Puffin.

READ THE OTHER ADVENTURES OF FELUDA IN PUFFIN

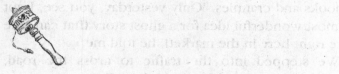

CHAPTER 1

'Nowhere in this country,' said Lalmohan Babu—alias Jatayu—in an admiring tone, 'will you find a market like our New Market!'

Feluda and I were in full agreement. Some time ago, there had been talk of pulling it down to build a modern multi-storey supermarket in its place. This had seriously upset Feluda.

'Don't they realize,' I had heard him fume, 'that if New Market is destroyed, it would mean the destruction of the very spirit of Calcutta? If they do go ahead, I hope the citizens will not hesitate to take to the streets in protest!' Luckily, the proposal was dropped.

We were now standing opposite New Market, having just seen *Ape and Superape* at the Globe. Lalmohan Babu needed batteries for his torch and a refill for his ballpoint pen. Feluda wanted a packet of daalmut from Kalimuddi's shop. Besides, Lalmohan Babu wanted to go around the whole market to inspect its nooks and crannies. 'Only yesterday, you see, I got the most wonderful idea for a ghost story that can take place right here in the market!' he told me.

We stepped into the traffic to cross the road, making our way carefully through endless private cars and taxis. Lalmohan Babu began to give me the details of his plot. 'There is this man, you see, a retired judge. One day, he comes to this market in the evening and discovers, a few hours later, that he can't get out! All shops are closed, all lights have been switched off, and he just can't find an exit. Every dark corridor is empty, except for an old antique shop in a small, narrow alley. There is only a flickering light in this shop. This man runs towards the shop, in the hope of finding help. Just as he reaches it, an arm comes out of the darkness. It is the arm of a skeleton, a dagger clutched in its hand, dripping with blood. It is the skeleton of a murderer, on whom the judge had once passed a death sentence. He has come back to take his revenge. The judge starts running blindly through the dark corridors, but it's no use. No matter how fast he runs or where he goes, he can still see the skeleton's arm, getting closer . . . . and closer.'

Not bad, I thought quietly to myself; an idea like this certainly had possibilities, although I was sure he'd have to appeal to Feluda for help, if only to produce a plausible explanation for the retired judge getting locked in.

We had, by now, come into the market. In front of us was a shop selling electrical goods. Lalmohan Babu could buy his batteries there and a refill for his pen from the shop opposite.

The owner of Dey Electricals knew Feluda. He greeted us with a smile. We were followed almost immediately by another man—about forty years of age, medium height, a receding hairline, wearing a white bush-shirt and black trousers. In his hand was a plastic bag.

'You're Mr Mitter, aren't you?' he asked.

'Yes, that's right.'

'A man in that book shop over there pointed you out. "The famous investigator, Pradosh Mitter," he said. It was really strange because I have been thinking of you for the last couple of days.'

'Really? Why?'

The man cleared his throat. Was he feeling nervous for some reason? 'I'll explain later if you allow me to call on you,' he said. 'Will you be home tomorrow?'

'Yes, but only after 5 p.m.'

'Very well. May I please have your address?' He took out a notebook and a fountain pen from his pocket, and handed them over to Feluda. Feluda wrote down our address and returned the notebook and pen to the gentleman. 'Sorry,' he said, looking ruefully at Feluda's finger, which was slightly smeared with violet ink. His pen was obviously leaking. 'My name is Batra,' he added.

Lalmohan Babu had gone to buy a refill. He returned just as Mr Batra left. 'Have you found yourself a client

3

already?' he asked. Feluda smiled, but did not say anything. The three of us came out, and began walking in the direction of the daalmut shop. Lalmohan Babu took out a red notebook and began scribbling in it. This meant, inevitably, that he got left behind each time he stopped to make a note. Then he had to rush forward to catch up with us. Feluda was walking in silence, looking straight ahead, but I knew his eyes and ears were taking in every detail.

The market was very crowded today, possibly because Puja was just round the corner. Lalmohan Babu said something about the crowd. I only caught the word 'cosmopolitan', but couldn't ask him to repeat what he had said, for we had arrived at Kalimuddi's shop. 'Salaam, Babu,' he said and began making up a packet for us. He knew what we wanted. I loved watching the way he mixed all the masala, shaking the packet gently. Its contents, I knew, would taste heavenly.

He finished in a few moments and passed the packet to me. Feluda put his hand into his pocket to take out his wallet, and turned into a statue. What on earth was the matter? What was he staring at? Had his wallet been stolen?

It took me a moment to realize what it was. Feluda's wallet was quite safe, but he was still staring at the man who had just walked past us, glancing once in our direction without the slightest sign of recognition. He looked exactly like Mr Batra.

'Twins,' whispered Lalmohan Babu.

I felt inclined to agree with him. Only an identical twin could bear such a startling resemblance. The only difference was that this man was wearing a dark blue shirt. And, of course, he didn't seem to know Feluda at all.

'There's nothing to feel so amazed about, really,' Feluda remarked. 'So what if Mr Batra has a twin? Dozens of people do!'

'No, sir,' said Lalmohan Babu most emphatically, 'if a mountain doesn't have a snow-capped peak, I don't call that a mountain at all.'

He was sitting in our living room the next evening, talking idly about going to a hill station for a holiday. There was an atlas lying on the coffee table. Lalmohan Babu stretched out a hand towards it, possibly to find the map of India, but withdrew it as the bell rang.

Srinath answered the door and, a minute later, Mr Batra walked in. Srinath followed, only a few moments later, with a cup of tea.

'Do you have a twin?' Lalmohan Babu asked as soon as Mr Batra was seated. His eyebrows shot up immediately, and his mouth fell open.

'How . . . how did you . . . ?'

'Let me explain,' Feluda said. 'We saw your twin soon after we met you yesterday in New Market.'

'Mr Mitter!' Mr Batra cried, bringing his fist down on the arm of his chair in excitement. 'I am the only child of my parents. I have no brother or sister.'

'Well, then—?'

'That is precisely why I've come to see you. It started a week ago, in Kathmandu. I work in a travel agency there called Sun Travels. I am their PRO. There is a good restaurant near my office where I have lunch every day. Last Monday, when I went there, the waiter said he was surprised to see me, for hadn't I already eaten my lunch? A couple of other people also said they had seen me eating only half an hour ago. Just imagine, Mr Mitter! It took me some time to convince them that the man they had seen wasn't me. Then the waiter said he had felt a little suspicious since this other man had a full lunch with rice and curry and everything, whereas I normally have a few sandwiches and a cup of coffee.' Mr Batra paused to take a sip from his cup. Then he continued, 'I arrived in Calcutta the day before yesterday, which was a Sunday. My work is such that I have to travel to Calcutta, Delhi and Bombay quite often. Anyway, yesterday, I was walking out of the hotel—I'm staying at the Grand—to buy some aspirin, when I heard someone say, "Mr Batra, can you come here for a minute?" It turned out to be a salesman from the hotel's gift shop. I went in, and he showed me a hundred rupee note. "This is a fake," he said, "there's no water mark on it. Please change it, sir." At first, I could only stare at him. You see, I hadn't been to that shop at all. But the salesman assured me that I—or someone who looked like me—had bought a kukri from them and given them that fake note!'

'Kukri? You mean a Nepali knife?' Lalmohan Babu asked.

'Yes. Why should I buy a Nepali knife here in Calcutta, tell me? I live in Nepal, for heaven's sake! I could buy a kukri any day at half the price.'

'Did you have to change the note?'

'Oh yes. I tried telling them I wasn't the same man, but they began to give me such strange looks that I . . .'

'Hm.'

'What am I to do, Mr Mitter?'

Feluda flicked the ash from his Charminar into an ashtray and said, 'I can understand how you must feel.'

'I am getting into a state of panic, Mr Mitter. God knows what this man will do next.'

'Yes, it's an awkward situation,' said Feluda slowly. I might have found it difficult to believe your story if I hadn't seen your lookalike myself. But even so, Mr Batra, I must confess I'm at a loss to see how I can help you.'

Mr Batra nodded, looking profoundly miserable. 'Yes, I know there's nothing for you to do—yet,' he said. 'My problem is that I am going back to Kathmandu tomorrow. What if this man follows me there? It's obvious he's trying to harass me deliberately. So far it's cost me only a hundred rupees, but who knows what he might do next? What if—?'

'Look,' Feluda interrupted gently, 'at this point of time I really cannot help you. Go straight to the police if you're harassed again in Kathmandu. What a man like this needs is a sound thrashing, and the police can hand it out much better than anyone else. But let us hope it won't come to that.'

'Yes, I certainly hope so,' said Mr Batra, rising to his feet. 'Anyway, at least this gave me the chance to meet you. I had heard such a lot about you from Sarweshwar Sahai.'

Sarweshwar Sahai was an old client.

'Goodbye, Mr Batra. Good luck!'

'Thank you, I may well need it. Goodbye!'

Lalmohan Babu was the first to speak after Mr Batra had gone.

'Strange!' he said. 'Kathmandu is a hill station! Why didn't I think of it before? Just because it's in a foreign country?'

CHAPTER 2

What happened the next day marked the real beginning of this story. But before I talk about it, I must mention the telephone call Feluda received a few hours after Mr Batra's departure.

Lalmohan Babu left at 7 p.m. 'It looks as though it's going to rain,' he said, looking out of the window. 'I had better be going today. Tell you what, Tapesh, I'll come back tomorrow. You see, I've thought some more about that new plot. I'd like to discuss it with you.'

It began to pour at around eight. The phone call came at 8.45. Feluda took it on the extension in his room. I heard the conversation on the main telephone in the living room.

'Mr Pradosh Mitter?' asked a deep, rather refined voice.

'Speaking.'

'You're the private investigator?'

'Yes.'

'Namaskar. My name is Anikendra Som. I'm calling from the Central Hotel.'

'Yes?'

'I need to meet you personally. When can I—?'

'Is it urgent?'

'Yes, very. It's raining so heavily it might be difficult to go out tonight, but I'd be grateful if you could find some time tomorrow morning. I've travelled to Calcutta expressly to meet you. I think you'll be interested in the reason.'

'I don't suppose you could explain a bit further on the telephone?'

'No, I'm sorry.'

'All right. How about nine o'clock tomorrow?'

'That's fine. Thank you.'

Mr Som rang off. Two clients in one evening, I thought to myself. At this rate, Feluda would soon have a queue outside our front door!

I had recently decided to follow Feluda's example and started to do yoga in the morning. We were both ready for the day by 8 a.m. Lalmohan Babu rang at half-past eight.

'I'm on my way to your house,' he said. 'I'll stop on the way at New Market to look at a green jerkin I saw the other day. I need to find out its price.' He had clearly started making preparations for going to a hill station.

More than an hour later, we were still waiting in the living room, but there was no sign of Mr Som. At 9.45, Feluda glanced at his watch and shook his head irritably. I could tell he was about to comment bitterly on Mr Som's sense of punctuality. But the telephone rang before he could utter a word.

'Why do I find your phone number in the diary of a murder victim?' boomed a familiar voice. It was Inspector Mahim Dattagupta, in charge of the Jorasanko police station.

Feluda frowned. 'Who's been murdered?'

'Come to Central Avenue, Central Hotel. Room number 23. All will be revealed.'

'Is it Anikendra Som?'

'Did you know him?'

'No, I was supposed to meet him this morning. How did he die?'

'Stabbed.'

'When?'

'Early this morning. I'll give you the details when you get here. I arrived about twenty minutes ago.'

'I'll try to get there in half an hour' said Feluda.

Lalmohan Babu walked in five minutes later, but did not get the chance to sit down. 'Murder,' said Feluda briefly, pushing him out of the house. Then he threw him into the back seat of his Ambassador, got in beside him and said to Lalmohan Babu's driver, 'Haripada, Central Hotel. Quickly.'

I got in the front with a swift glance at Lalmohan Babu's face. Shock and bewilderment were writ large, but he knew Feluda wouldn't tell him anything even if he asked.

Haripada drove as fast as the traffic let him. Inspector Dattagupta filled us in when we arrived. Apparently, Anikendra Som had checked in on Sunday evening. The hotel register showed he lived in Kanpur. He was supposed to check out tomorrow. At 5 a.m. this morning, a man came and asked for him. On being given his room number, the man went up, using the stairs, not the lift. He was seen leaving the hotel fifteen minutes later. The hotel staff who had seen him described him as a man of medium height, clean-shaven, clad in a blue bush-shirt and grey trousers. The chowkidar said he had a taxi waiting.

Mr Som had ordered breakfast at 8 a.m. A waiter arrived on the dot, but when there was no response to his loud knocking, he opened the door with a duplicate key. He found Mr Som's body sprawled on the floor, stabbed in the chest with a kukri. The knife had not been removed.

In due course, the police arrived and searched the room. All they found was a small VIP suitcase with a few clothes in it, and a pair of boots. There was no sign of a wallet or money or any other valuables. Presumably, the killer had removed everything. Feluda went in to have a look at the body. 'A good-looking man,' he told us afterwards. 'Couldn't have been more than thirty.'

According to the receptionist, Mr Som had spent most of his time outside the hotel the day before. He had returned an hour before it started raining. Since the rooms did not have telephones, he had used the telephone directory at the reception desk to look up a number. Then he had written it down in his notebook and used the telephone at the reception counter to make a call.

The police found the notebook with Feluda's number in it. It was lying on the floor between the bed and the bedside table. Only the first three pages had been written on. There were disjointed sentences, apparently written at random.

'What do you make of this?' Feluda asked, showing me the scribbles.

'Well, it looks as though a rather shaky hand wrote these words. The word "den", in particular, is almost illegible.'

'Perhaps the man was under terrible mental strain,' remarked Lalmohan Babu.

'Maybe. Or he may have been travelling at enormous speed. I think those words were written in an aeroplane, and as he was writing the word "den", the plane dropped into an air pocket.'

'Yes, you must be right!' exclaimed Lalmohan Babu. 'Awful things, air pockets. I remember on our way to Bombay, I had just taken a sip from my cup of coffee when there was such a mighty bump that I choked and spluttered . . . God, it was awful!'

Feluda wrote the words down in his own notebook and returned Mr Som's to the inspector.

'I will inform his people in Kanpur,' said Mahim Babu. 'The body will have to be identified.'

'I believe there is an evening flight from Delhi that comes via Kanpur. You can check if the passenger list last Sunday had Mr Som's name on it. But I think he had recently been to a hilly area.'

'Why, what makes you say that?'

'Did you notice those heavy boots in that corner? One of them has a piece of fern stuck on its heel. It couldn't have come from a place on the plains.'

'Yes, you're probably right. I'll keep you informed, Mr Mitter, especially if we find any fingerprints on the kukri.'

'There's one other thing. Please check with the gift shop in the Grand Hotel if the kukri was sold by them.'

On our way back, Feluda showed us the words he had found in Mr Som's notebook:

1. Is it only LSD?
2. Ask CP about methods and past cases.
3. Den—is it here or there?
4. Find out about AB.
5. Ring up PCM, DDC.

The last sentence was followed by Feluda's number.

'Is it something to do with foreign exchange?' asked Lalmohan Babu.

'Why do you say that?'

'Well, LSD . . . I mean, it looks like an L, but could it be pound-shillings-pence?'

Feluda clicked his tongue in mock annoyance. 'Do stop thinking of money all the time,' he admonished. 'This LSD refers to the drug, Lysergic Acid Diethylamide. The whole world knows about it. The human brain contains a chemical called serotonin, which helps the brain function normally. LSD, I believe, reduces the level of this chemical. The brain then acts abnormally, causing hallucinations. For instance, if you took a dose of the drug now and looked out of the window, you wouldn't see the traffic or the crowds. Green meadows and rippling rivers may greet your eyes instead.'

'Really? Is it possible to buy this stuff?'

'Yes, it most certainly is; but not, obviously, at your local pharmacy. It is sold secretly. If you went to the hotel behind the Globe cinema where a lot of hippies stay, you might be lucky enough to get a sugar cube.'

'Sugar cube?'

'Yes. Just one grain of LSD in a sugar cube is quite enough. It would have the strength of—to borrow your own phrase—five thousand horsepower! But, mind you, hallucinations caused by this drug needn't necessarily be beautiful. I have heard of a case where a man climbed to the roof of a multi-storey building and threw himself over, thinking all the while that he was simply going down a flight of stairs'

'My God! You mean—?'

'Yes. Instant death.'

'How terrible!'

CHAPTER 3

Two days after the murder, Inspector Dattagupta rang Feluda. He had a lot to say.

Anikendra Som, it turned out, used to teach at the Kanpur IIT. He had no family there, but the police had located a brother in Calcutta, who had identified the body. Apparently, Mr Som was a loner. He was barely in touch with his relations, although his brother agreed that he had always been a brave and honest man.

Secondly, there were no fingerprints on the kukri. But it was possible to tell from the way it had been used that the murderer was left-handed. The shop in the Grand Hotel had confirmed that the weapon had indeed been sold by them, to one Mr Batra. He was staying in the hotel and had left for Kathmandu by the nine o'clock flight the same morning Mr Som was killed.

Finally, Anikendra Som's name could not be found on the list of passengers on the flight from Kanpur. However, the police had checked the passenger lists of all other flights that came in on Sunday, and discovered that Mr Som's name featured on the Kathmandu-Calcutta flight. It had reached Dum Dum at 5.30 p.m.

Mahim Babu finished by saying, 'Since the culprit seems to have escaped to Nepal, there's nothing we can do from here. The case will have to be passed on to the CID (homicide), and the Home Department. Once the Home Department gives the go-ahead, the Government of Nepal can be requested to help with inquiries. If they agree, a man from the CID will travel to Kathmandu.'

Feluda said only one thing before replacing the receiver, 'Best of luck!'

Feluda sank into silence after this and, for the next couple of days, said virtually nothing. But I could tell that he was thinking deeply and trying to work something out, from the way he paced in his room, cracking his knuckles absentmindedly, and occasionally throwing himself on his bed, only to stare at the ceiling.

On the second day, Lalmohan Babu arrived in the evening and stayed for nearly two hours, but Feluda did not utter a single word. In the end, Lalmohan Babu told me what he had come to say.

'You know what, Tapesh,' he began, 'I've just been to see a palmist. His name is Moulinath Bhattacharya. An amazing man. He doesn't just read palms, but also does his own research. And his theories are fantastic. According to him, monkeys, like human beings, have lines on their palms and it is possible to read them. So he spoke to the curator of the local zoo and actually went into the cage of a chimpanzee. Apparently, it was a very well-mannered and well-trained animal. Mouli Babu took ten minutes to look carefully at his palms, but he didn't seem to mind at all. Only, as Mouli Babu turned to go, the chimp stretched out a hand and pulled his trousers down. But that might have been an accident, don't you think? Anyway, Mouli Babu says this animal will live until August 1983. I've noted the date down in my diary. Thrilling, isn't it?'

'Yes' I said. 'If his prediction comes true, it will be remarkable. But what did he tell you about yourself?'

'Oh, something very interesting. Five years ago, another palmist had told me I'd never travel abroad. Mouli Babu said I would, most definitely.'

As things turned out, Lalmohan Babu was not disappointed. Feluda broke his silence the next day, saying over breakfast, 'Do you know what my heart's been telling me, Topshe? It keeps saying all roads lead to Nepal. And some of them are long and winding. So I think it's time for Felu Mitter to pay a visit to Kathmandu.'

It took us three days to make all the arrangements. The three of us were booked on an Indian Airlines flight. Our travel agent also made hotel reservations in Kathmandu.

'Do you think Batra number two has returned to Kathmandu?' I asked Feluda one day.

'Possibly. You heard what Mahim Babu said. If a criminal manages to escape to another country, he can be quite safe until the two governments come to an agreement. And that can take ages. Criminals in the USA try to cross the border into Mexico. It's the same story between India and Nepal.'

Lalmohan Babu turned up the day before we were to leave to say that he had seen the 'fake' Mr Batra near Lenin Sarani, having a glass of lassi.

Feluda's eyes narrowed.

'Was he holding the glass in his left hand?' he asked.

'Eh heh—I didn't notice that!'

'In that case, your statement has no value at all.'

The officer who checked us in at the airport happened to know Feluda. 'I'll give you seats on the right,' he said. 'You'll get a good view.'

But I had no idea just how good the view could be. Within ten minutes of leaving Calcutta, I could see Kanchenjunga glittering on our right—a sight as rare as it was breathtaking. This was followed by glimpses of several other famous peaks, each of which, I knew, held an irresistible attraction for adventurous mountaineers.

We were still looking out of the window, transfixed, when an air hostess stopped by Feluda's seat and said, 'Captain Mukherjee, the pilot, would like to see you in the cockpit.' Feluda unfastened his seat belt and stood up. 'Can my friends go too, when I get back?' he asked.

The air hostess smiled. 'Why don't all of you come with me?' she said.

The cockpit was too small for us all to get inside, but what I saw from the top of Feluda's shoulder was enough to make me give an involuntary gasp. Lalmohan Babu was peering from the other side. He later described his feeling as one of 'speechless, breathless, enchanting, captivating wonder'.

A row of peaks formed a wall in the distance. The closer we got, the bigger they seemed. The co-pilot laid aside the paperback he had been reading and began to point these peaks out to us. After Kanchenjunga came Makalu, and a little later, we saw Mount Everest. Then came Gourishankar, Annapurna and Dhaulagiri.

We returned to our seats in five minutes. In less than half an hour, I could sense that the plane was losing height. I looked out of the window again and saw a thick green carpet spread below. This must be the famous Terai. The Kathmandu Valley lay behind this.

At this point, we disappeared into a grey mist and the plane started bumping up and down. Luckily, the mist cleared only a few minutes later, the plane steadied itself, and we caught our first glimpse of a beautiful valley, bathed in sunlight.

'One doesn't have to be told this is a foreign country!' exclaimed Lalmohan Babu, swallowing hard.

True. I had never seen anything like this in India. There were trees and rivers and rice fields and houses—but, somehow, everything seemed different.

'Look at those little houses' said Feluda. 'They're made of bricks, with roofs thatched with straw. They were built by the Chinese.'

'And what are those? Temples?'

'Yes, Buddhist temples.'

I now noticed the shadow of our plane on the ground. Suddenly, it began to grow larger and larger, until it seemed to shoot up in the air and disappear. We had landed at Tribhuvan airport.

CHAPTER 4

We had been warned that customs officials in Nepal were very strict. Apparently, every single passenger was required to have all his baggage examined.

Lalmohan Babu, I noticed, was looking somewhat uneasy. This surprised me since I knew none of us was carrying anything suspicious. On being questioned, he said, 'I brought a little aam papad in a tiffin box. Suppose they object?'

They didn't. Lalmohan Babu relaxed, turned towards the exit, and froze. I followed his gaze and saw why. One of the two Batras was standing near the door, talking to a tall, white man with a beard.

It turned out to be the real Mr Batra. His face broke into a smile as he caught sight of Feluda. He said 'Excuse me' to his companion and came forward to greet us.

'Welcome to Kathmandu!' he said.

'I felt I had to come,' Feluda explained.

'Very good, very good.' Mr Batra shook our hands. I don't think that other man followed me back here. There hasn't been any problem in the last few days. How long are you here for?'

'About a week.'

'Where are you staying?'

'Hotel Lumbini.'

'It's a new hotel, and quite good. If you want to go sightseeing, I can make all the arrangements for you. My office is only five minutes from your hotel.'

'Thank you. By the way, do you get Indian newspapers here? Did you see this?' Feluda took out a cutting from the *Statesman* and handed it to Mr Batra. It was a report on the murder of Mr Som. Mr Batra read it quickly, then looked up, his eyes filled with apprehension.

'What that report does not say,' Feluda told him, 'is that a man called Batra bought that Nepali kukri from the shop in the Grand Hotel. The police had this verified.'

'Oh my God! ' Mr Batra went very pale.

'You didn't know Anikendra Som, did you?'

'No, never heard of him.'

'He travelled on the same plane as you.'

'From Kathmandu? Nepal Airlines?'

'Yes.'

'Then maybe I'd have recognized him if I saw him, although—mind you—there were a hundred and thirty passengers on that flight.'

'Yes. Anyway, try and stay away from Calcutta for the moment,' Feluda said lightly.

'But why should anyone try to harass me like this, Mr Mitter?' Mr Batra wailed.

'Well, I can think of a good reason,' Feluda said slowly. 'If a criminal discovers that he has a lookalike, isn't it natural for him to try and frame the other man, so that he himself can get away scot-free?'

'All right, but this is no ordinary crime, Mr Mitter. We're talking of murder!'

'I am convinced, Mr Batra, that the killer will return to Kathmandu. Anikendra Som had gone to Calcutta to seek my help. I do not know what he wanted me to do, but I won't rest in peace until I've caught the man who murdered him. So if you, or anyone you know, sees this man who looks like you, I hope you'll let me know immediately.'

'Oh yes, certainly. I have to go out of town tomorrow, but I'll contact you the day after.'

We came out of the airport and got into a taxi. It was a Japanese Datsun, one of the many that could be seen on the clean, broad, beautiful roads of Kathmandu. Eucalyptus trees stood in neat rows by the sides of these roads. We passed a large park with a stadium in it. There were huge buildings everywhere, many of which had once been palaces owned by the Ranas. Some among them were Hindu and Buddhist temples, their spires towering over everything else.

It was easy to see from the way Lalmohan Babu was rubbing his hands that he was already quite impressed by what he had seen in this foreign land. When Feluda told him that the king of Nepal was the only Hindu king in the world, and that Lumbini, where Lord Buddha was born, was in Nepal, his mouth parted and formed a silent 'O'.

Our taxi drove down Kanti Path and passed through a large and elaborately carved gate. A right turn brought us into New Road. Hotel Lumbini, together with many other hotels and rest houses, stood on one side of this road. Our taxi drew up near its front door.

The first man we met as we were checking in turned out to be a Bengali. He rose from a sofa and came forward to greet us.

'Did you come by the Indian Airlines flight?' he addressed Lalmohan Babu.

'Yes'

'Is this your first visit to Nepal?'

'Yes. We're on holiday' Lalmohan Babu replied with a sidelong glance at Feluda.

'You must visit Pokhara, if you can.'

This time, Feluda spoke.

'Do you live here?' he asked. A bell boy, in the meantime, had taken our luggage upstairs. We were given two adjacent rooms on the second floor, numbers 226 and 227.

'I am from Calcutta. I've come on a holiday with my family. My friend here lives in Kathmandu.'

I noticed for the first time that another elderly gentleman was sitting on the sofa. His skin was very fair, and his hair totally white. He was distinguished looking. He now rose and joined us.

'His family has lived here for three hundred years,' the first gentleman told us.

'What!'

'Yes, you must get him to tell you his story.'

'Well, if you don't mind, why don't you come up to our room and join us for a cup of tea?' said Feluda. 'I am interested in Bengalis living in Nepal . . . for a specific reason, you see.'

I knew exactly what he meant. I also knew that Feluda didn't normally invite people up to his room so soon after being introduced to them.

Feluda and I had been given a double room. All of us trooped into it, and Feluda rang room service for tea. Our guests formally introduced themselves. The gentleman from Calcutta was called Mr Bhowmik. The other gentleman was Mr Harinath Chakravarty. Over a cup of tea, he related the history of his family.

Nearly three hundred years ago, Nepal had been struck by a severe drought. The Mallyas were then the rulers. King Jagatjit Mallya invited a tantrik from Bengal, to see if his magical powers could bring rain. This tantrik was Harinath's ancestor, Jairam Chakravarty. Jairam did some special puja, as a result of which it rained in the Kathmandu Valley for eleven continuous days. After this, Jagatjit Mallya could not allow him to go back. He gave him land to live on, and made sure that Jairam and his family lived in comfort.

When the Mallyas were ousted by the Ranas, Jairam continued to be looked after, for the Ranas were orthodox Hindus. Until two generations ago, the men of the Chakravarty family lived as priests of the royal household. An uncle of Harinath was still a priest in the temple of Pashupatinath. It was his father who was the first in the family to go to Calcutta for higher studies. He returned to work as a private tutor for the Ranas. Harinath himself did the same. He went to Calcutta to study English literature. When he came back to Nepal, the Ranas appointed him as private tutor. But, over a period of time, the Ranas lost their power. When, eventually, a college opened in Kathmandu in the name of Raja Tribhuvan, Harinath joined it as a professor of English.

'My sons, of course,' said Harinath Babu, bringing his tale to an end, 'were not even remotely interested in priesthood. The older, Niladri, used to work as a trainer in the mountaineering institute.'

'Used to? I mean—?'

'He died in a climbing accident in 1976.'

'I'm sorry. What about your other children?'

'I had another son, Himadri. He worked as a helicopter pilot. Took tourists to look at the Terai and the famous Himalayan peaks. I . . . I lost him too. Only three weeks ago.'

'Air crash?'

Harinath Babu shook his head sadly. 'No. That would have made sense. What really happened was weird. He had taken a friend to look at a monastery. When he returned, he found a small injury on his hand. He had no idea how he had got it, but his friend thought it might have been caused by barbed wire. Himadri tried to shrug it off, but his friend insisted on calling a doctor to give him an anti-tetanus shot.'

'What happened then?'

Harinath Babu shook his head again. 'Nothing. The shot didn't help. He got tetanus and died.'

'Perhaps by the time he was given the shot, it was already too late?'

'No, I don't think so. According to the friend, he cut his hand in the evening. The shot was given the following morning. But he began to have convulsions soon after that. We lost him the same day.'

'The doctor who was called . . . was he your own?'

'No, but I know him. It was Dr Divakar. He has quite a large practice. It seems to have grown since our family physician, Dr Mukherjee, died. Dr Divakar is now a fairly wealthy man.'

Mr Bhowmik spoke suddenly. 'Never mind about the doctor,' he said. 'It is the drug that must be questioned. It's not unusual at all these days, is it, for a patient to die because of a spurious drug? They put water in ampoules, talcum powder in capsules, or powdered chalk, or just plain dust. Surely you've heard of this before?'

Harinath Babu gave a wan smile. Yes. But what could I do? I had to accept the situation. My son was dead. That was that.'

The two gentlemen rose to leave.

'I am afraid I have wasted a lot of your time,' said Harinath Babu.

'Not at all,' Feluda replied. 'There is only one thing I'd like to ask.'

'Yes?'

'Is it possible to meet your son's friend?'

'No, I'm afraid not. He was staying at our house. He had been profoundly shocked by Himadri's death. I tried to comfort him by saying it was destiny, no one was to blame. But this seemed to upset him even more. He stopped speaking to me. Then, a week after my son's death, he left our house without a word. I do not know where he went. But he's bound to come back sooner or later, for we've still got most of his things.'

'What is his name?'

'Anikendra Som. We call him Anik.'

CHAPTER 5

Half an hour later, we had had a shower and were down at the hotel's restaurant, Nirvana, to have lunch. I had not expected things to move quite so quickly so soon after our arrival. Mr Som's murder in Calcutta, Himadri Chakravarty's death in Kathmandu, the fake Mr Batra—all these were undoubtedly linked together. Had Mr Som wanted Feluda to investigate the death of his friend? Did he really die because he was injected with a spurious drug?

A waiter arrived to take our order. Lalmohan Babu peered at the menu and asked, 'What is mo-mo?'

'It's meat balls in sauce, sir,' the waiter replied.

'It's a Tibetan dish,' Feluda told him. 'Try it, Lalmohan Babu. When you go back to Calcutta, you can tell your friends you ate the same thing as the Dalai Lama.'

'OK, one mo-mo for me, please.'

The waiter finished taking our order and left. Lalmohan Babu now produced a light green card.

'A man at the counter handed this to me,' he said, 'but, for the life of me, I can't figure out what to do with it. I can recognize the word "casino", but what's all this? Jackpot, pontoon, roulette, blackjack . . . and, look, it says its value is five dollars. What does it mean?'

Feluda explained, 'There is a very famous hotel here, which has a big casino for gambling. Those words that you read out are names of various types of gambling. Gambling in public isn't permitted in our country, so you won't find a casino in any Indian hotel. What you can do with that card is show it at the casino and try your hand at any game. You can spend up to five dollars without paying anything from your own pocket.'

'Hey, that sounds interesting! Why don't we . . . ?'

'I don't mind!' I said.

'Yes. How can a horse resist a carrot if it dangles right before its nose? What do you say, Felu Babu?'

'Horse? You may well feel like an ass when you've finished. But then, if you're lucky enough, who knows what might happen?'

We decided to spend an evening at the casino. Our hotel would arrange transport, at no extra cost.

Our food arrived. Delicious!' said Lalmohan Babu, tasting his mo-mo. 'I must get the recipe from somewhere. I have an excellent cook back home who, I'm sure, could make it for me. Six months of consuming this stuff and one is bound to start looking distinguished.'

We went out after lunch. 'Let's go to Darbar Square,' said Feluda. 'That is where the main police station is. I must go there. The two of you can look around, then meet me somewhere.'

Darbar Square startled us all. It reminded me of a chessboard, when a game is well under way. Just as the board is littered with chessmen in various positions, the square was strewn with palaces, temples, statues and pillars. Amidst these, hundreds of people went about their business, and traffic flowed endlessly. In a distant way, it was a bit like Varanasi. But in Varanasi, all famous temples were hidden in narrow lanes. Here, the roads were so much wider. The old royal palace had a huge open space in front of it. It must have held a vast number of people when the king used to stand on a balcony to grant an audience.

Feluda consulted a map. 'If you go straight, you'll soon find the statue of Kaal Bhairav. I'll meet you there in half an hour.' He strode away.

Lalmohan Babu and I began walking. I was struck by the amazing carvings on the wooden doors, windows and even roofs of old buildings. I had heard Nepal was famous for its woodwork. Now I could see why. There were a few Hindu temples, built in a style similar to those in India. And there were pagodas, built in several layers, each layer getting narrower as one moved to the top.

However, Darbar Square wasn't just a place for religion. There was a large market, spread all over.

Every imaginable object from vegetables to garments was being sold on pavements, corridors and stairs. Lalmohan Babu and I stopped at a small stall selling rather attractive Nepali caps. He brought out his little red notebook again.

I found a nice cap for myself, and had just started bargaining over its price, when Lalmohan Babu nudged me. 'Tapesh!' he whispered. I turned around and found him staring at something, transfixed.

A few yards away stood one of the two Batras. He was in the process of lighting a cigarette. Then he walked away, without looking at us.

'Have you ever seen your cousin use a lighter with his left hand?'

'No.'

'This man did.'

'Yes, I saw him. Then he put it in his left pocket.'

'Should we follow him?'

'Do you think he saw you?'

'No.'

'OK, let's go.'

We didn't have to meet Feluda for another twenty minutes. The two of us leapt forward.

There was a temple in front of us. The man seemed to have disappeared in the crowd. But we saw him again once we had left the temple behind us. He was going into a lane. We followed, keeping a distance of about twenty yards between us.

There were small shops and restaurants on both sides of the lane. Many had 'Pie Shop' written on their signboards. I could smell food everywhere. A group of hippies came strolling by. As they walked past us, the smell of food was momentarily drowned by that of ganja, sweat and unwashed clothes.

'Oh no!' said Lalmohan Babu. The man had gone into a shop to our right.

What should we do now? Should we wait for him to come out? What if he took a long time? We had only fifteen minutes to spare.

'Let's go into the shop,' I said. 'He doesn't know us. We're quite safe.'

'Yes, you're right.'

We stepped in. It was a shop selling Tibetan handicrafts. There was a counter facing the front door. Behind it was another open door, leading to a dark room. The second Mr Batra must have slipped into this room, for he was nowhere to be seen. 'Yes?' said a voice. I now noticed a Tibetan lady standing behind the counter, smiling politely. By her side sat an old man with a withered and wrinkled face. He appeared to be dozing.

Obviously, we had to pretend we had come in to buy something. There were certainly plenty of things to choose from—masks, tankhas, prayer wheels, brassware, statues.

'I like mo-mo,' Lalmohan Babu declared, for no apparent reason.

'I am sorry, sir, but that's something you'll get in a restaurant, not here,' the lady replied.

'No, no, no,' Lalmohan Babu shook his head vigorously. 'I don't want to eat it.'

The lady raised her light eyebrows. 'I thought you just said you liked it!'

'No. Yes, I mean—not now. What I want now—
I mean—'

I raised a hand to stop him. 'Do you have a Tibetan
cookbook?' I asked, knowing very well they didn't.

'Sorry,' said the lady.

We said 'Thank you' quickly and came out. There
was nothing to do now but go tamely back the way
we had come, and find the statue of Kaal Bhairav. We
stopped on the way briefly to buy a couple of Nepali
caps.

What a horrifying statue it was! It gave me the
creeps in broad daylight. Heaven knew how people felt
if they saw it at night.

Feluda arrived five minutes later. The main entrance
to the police station was right opposite the statue. We
both were dying to tell him about our little adventure,
but I was curious to learn why he had gone to the
police station in the first place. 'I just met the OC,
Mr Rajgurung. He said they'd cooperate in every way
if the Nepal government officially agreed to help. He
seemed a very nice man.'

'That man is here, Felu Babu,' Lalmohan Babu
blurted out. I explained fully.

'Are you sure you saw him light his cigarette with
his left hand?'

'Yes. We both saw him!'

'Very good,' said Feluda. 'We must inform Mr Batra
tomorrow. Look, why don't you carry on? I must go
back to the hotel right now to make a few phone calls.'

Something told me Feluda was not going to do
much sightseeing in Kathmandu.

CHAPTER 6

A right turn from the main crossing outside our hotel led to Shukra Path, which ran straight on to join a shopping complex. A large covered area stood packed with rows of small departmental stores. Each one of them sold imported stuff, ranging from clothes, watches, tape recorders, radios and calculators, to writing material, sweets and chocolates.

'I feel like howling!' Lalmohan Babu proclaimed, standing outside one of these shops.

'Why?'

'All these shops, dear boy, just look at all those goodies! They are not meant for people like us, are they? I'm sure all these shops are patronized by people like . . . like . . . .John D. Rockefeller, or superstars from Bombay, perhaps?'

In the end, however, he succumbed to temptation and bought two metres of light orange Japanese terrywool. 'I need new trousers,' he told me. The shop offered to have them tailored by 4 p.m. the next evening.

'That colour would be most apt for the Land of the Lamas, wouldn't you say?' he asked, emerging from the shop, looking immensely pleased. I didn't want to cast a damper, but felt obliged to point out that Nepal could hardly be called the Land of the Lamas, since eighty per cent of the population was Hindu.

We came back to the hotel to find Feluda scribbling in his notebook. 'Sit down,' he said. 'I've called a doctor.'

Doctor? Was he unwell?

We promptly sat on the sofa, fixing anxious eyes on him. Feluda took a couple of minutes to finish writing. Then he pushed aside the notebook and explained, I've called Dr Divakar, the same doctor who had given the tetanus injection to Himadri Chakravarty. He normally sees patients at the Star Dispensary on Dharma Path. I will, of course, have to pay him his fee, but that cannot be helped. I'd much rather talk to him here.'

'Drugs and medicines seem to play an important role in this investigation,' Lalmohan Babu observed.

'Not just important, Lalmohan Babu,' Feluda said. 'I believe that in this whole sad business, they play a crucial role.'

'What about that surgical acid Mr Som's notebook mentioned? Is it—'

'Lysergic acid, not surgical. But then—'

Feluda picked up his notebook again, frowning. 'The term LSD can mean something else. It occurred to me only a few minutes ago. You see, LSD could also stand for Life Saving Drugs, such as anti-tetanus serum, or things like penicillin, teramycin, streptomycin, drugs to fight TB and heart problems. I think,' Feluda glanced at his notebook, 'where it says "find out about AB", it's referring to these drugs. AB could mean antibiotics. Mr Som was clearly trying to find out more about these. "Ring up PCM, DDC"— well, PCM is Pradosh Chandra Mitter, and DDC is probably the Directorate of Drug Control. It's likely that Mr Som had a sample of a drug that he wanted people at Drug Control to test. It's amazing how methodically he was working. With a brain like that, he could have been a sleuth himself!'

'Didn't the letters "CP" feature somewhere?'

'That's easy. It stands for Calcutta Police. Here, it says "Ask CP about methods and past cases".'

'That would mean you've decoded everything—'

The door bell rang. I opened the door.

The man who walked in startled me somewhat, for I had never seen a doctor so impeccably dressed. His suit must have been made by the best tailor in Kathmandu. He wore glasses with gold frames. The watch on his wrist was obviously imported, and expensive. A gift from a grateful patient, perhaps?

Since Feluda was sitting on the bed, the doctor assumed he was the patient. He walked over to him and asked, 'What's wrong?' I offered him a chair. Feluda had risen, but at the doctor's question, sat down again. Then he took out an envelope from under his pillow and held it out. Here you are,' he said. Dr Divakar looked quite taken aback.

'What is this?'

'This contains your fee. And this is my visiting card.'

Dr Divakar sat down, looking curiously at Feluda's card.

'I realize I have some explaining to do,' Feluda went on, 'and I apologize for dragging you out like this. Allow me to tell you first of all that I am here to investigate a murder. It happened in Calcutta, but I have reason to believe the killer is in Kathmandu. I am trying to gather as much information as I can. I believe you can help me.'

Dr Divakar's brows were knitted in a frown. 'Who was murdered?' he asked.

'I'm coming to that. Please let me verify something first. Was it you who gave an anti-tetanus shot to Harinath Chakravarty's son, Himadri?'

'Yes, that's right.'

'Did the injection come from your own stock?'

'Yes, from my dispensary.'

'But it did not work, did it?'

'No, but surely you don't think I am responsi—'

'No, no, Dr Divakar, nobody's blaming you, or trying to establish who was responsible. After all, a case like this is, by no means, unique. Most people accept it quietly. Harinath Babu did the same. What I want to know is whether you, as a doctor, have any ideas or theories about the reason behind Himadri's death.'

'There may well be more than one reason,'
Dr Divakar replied. Firstly, Himadri couldn't tell me for
sure when he had cut his hand. His friend thought it
was about sixteen hours before they came to me. Now,
if his friend was wrong and it was twenty-six hours
instead of sixteen, then by the time that shot was given
it was too late. Secondly, no one knew whether he had
ever taken a preventive. If he had, the injection might
have worked. His father seemed to think he had, but
Himadri wasn't sure. Harinath Babu might have been
mistaken. After the death of his wife and the other son,
his memory, I have noticed, fails him at times.'

'All right. But did Himadri's friend take an ampoule
from your dispensary after he died?'

'Yes.'

'Anti-tetanus?'

'Yes'

'How do you know that? Did he speak to you?'

'No, he didn't just speak to me. He threatened me,
Mr Mitter. He said it was my fault that Himadri died.'

'It is this friend of Himadri's who has been killed.'

'What!'

'Yes. His name is Anikendra Som.'

Dr Divakar stared. Feluda went on, He took that
ampoule to Calcutta to have it analysed. He must've
been convinced that its contents were not genuine. But
I don't think he got the chance to contact a laboratory.
He wanted me to help him get to the bottom of this
business.'

'No drug that came from my dispensary could be
spurious,' said Dr Divakar firmly.

'How can you be so sure? Do you examine every ampoule before you give an injection?'

The doctor's face turned red. 'How is that possible, Mr Mitter? When a patient needs immediate attention in an emergency case, how can I waste time getting all my drugs tested?'

'Where do you get your medicines from?'

'From wholesalers. Each batch has a number, a date of expiry—'

'Don't you know these can be faked? Those involved in this racket have secret dealings with printers who print those labels. Numbers, dates, even names of well-known foreign pharmaceutical firms can be locally printed. Surely, you're not unaware of this?'

Dr Divakar looked as though he couldn't find a suitable reply.

'Listen, doctor,' Feluda said, his tone milder now, 'I give you my word no one will come to know of this. But I would like you to have an ampoule of your anti-tetanus injection tested. Then let me know what the lab says in its report. We haven't much time, as you know.'

Dr Divakar rose slowly and began walking towards the door. 'Tomorrow I have an urgent case to attend to. I shall contact you the day after,' he said.

'Thank you very much. Your help will be much appreciated.'

There was no doubt that we had got involved in a most complex affair. The more I saw, the more I began to respect Mr Som. Feluda would not allow his killer to escape, no matter who he was.

'Let's go for a walk,' said Feluda after dinner. I began to feel vaguely suspicious about his intent as he started walking in the direction of Darbar Square. My suspicions were confirmed when he stopped before the old royal palace and said, 'All right, then. Which lane was it?'

Darbar Square looked quite different at night. Bells pealed in temples; from somewhere came the strains of a Hindi song; and tourists and cycle rickshaws made walking difficult. We had to push our way through to find the right lane.

'The hippies would call it a pig alley,' remarked Feluda. We walked past the pie shops and finally found the shop selling handicrafts.

It was still open. A couple of customers were standing before the counter. The same lady stood behind it. The old man had gone.

Feluda ran his eyes over the building from outside. It had two floors. The shop was on the ground floor. There were two windows on the first floor facing the lane. Both were closed, but through a crack we could see a faint light.

Another narrow lane ran on the other side of the shop. A few yards down this lane stood a building with three storeys, with 'Heaven's Gate Lodge' written on its front door. Its appearance evoked no heavenly images, but it was clearly a hotel, situated rather conveniently near the Tibetan shop. We pushed open the door and went in.

'How much do you charge for rooms here?' Feluda asked.

'Ten for a single. Fifteen for a double,' replied the man sitting behind the reception desk. He was busy tapping at a calculator.

'Are any rooms available?'

'How many do you need?'

'A single and a double, please, preferably on the first floor. But we'd like to have a look first, if you don't mind.'

The receptionist rang a bell without a word. A Nepali bearer appeared. The gentleman handed him a key and motioned us on. He was obviously a man of few words.

We followed the bearer up a flight of stairs and down a long passage. He stopped before the last door on the right and unlocked it. We stepped into the room. One look at the window told me that our mission was successful. Through it we could see a portion of a room above the Tibetan store.

By the time Lalmohan Babu had inspected the room, tested the light switches, checked on the number of blankets and done everything possible to convince the bearer that we had indeed come to book the room, Feluda and I had seen what there was to see.

The old man from the shop was sitting in the dimly lit room. We could see only his head and shoulders. There was a pile of cardboard boxes behind him. His hands were busy either taking something out of the boxes, or packing something in them.

There was another man in the room, though all we got to see was his shadow. He was leaning over the old Tibetan, watching him work.

Suddenly, my heart skipped a beat.

The shadow took out a packet of cigarettes from its pocket, and placed a cigarette between its lips. Then it took out another object.

It was a lighter.

The shadow now lit the lighter.

With its left hand.

CHAPTER 7

'You two can do some more sightseeing today,' said
Feluda, the next morning after breakfast. 'Try and
see Swayambhu, Pashupatinath and Patan. That should
be enough for a day. Let's go to Sun Travels. They
should be able to arrange a car.'

We bumped into Mr Batra the minute we stepped out
of the hotel. This must be telepathy, I thought. He smiled
as he greeted us. But his face grew grave almost instantly.

'That man is back here,' he told us. 'A colleague
of mine saw him yesterday, coming out of a jeweller's
shop on New Road.'

'Did your colleague think you had returned
unexpectedly from Pokhara?'

Mr Batra smiled again. 'No, and I'll tell you why. You
see, my "twin" appears to be rather partial to bright
colours. Yesterday he was wearing a shocking pink

pullover and green shirt. People who know me well would never mistake him for me. But anyway, I went to the police and told them about it. I happen to know a sub-inspector.'

'What did he say?'

'I feel much reassured by what he said. Apparently, the police already know about this man. They think he's involved in smuggling, but is being protected by someone rich and influential. So the police can't actually do anything until he makes a false move.'

'Didn't you tell him about the inconvenience he has caused you? He did buy that kukri in your name, you know.'

'Yes, yes. I asked the sub-inspector if this man could commit a crime, and then get me framed. Do you know what the sub-inspector did? He burst out laughing. He said, "Please Mr Batra, don't think the Nepal Police are so stupid!"'

'Well, that's that, then. Surely now you're feeling a lot better?'

'Well, yes. I am much relieved, I must admit. And I think you should also relax a little. Why should you spend your entire stay in Kathmandu simply chasing a criminal? Tell you what, why don't you spend a day at the new forest bungalow our company has just built in the Rapti Valley, in the Terai? It's a really wonderful spot. I need only a few hours' notice to get a car to pick you up. In fact, if I happen to be free, I can join you myself. What do you say?'

The very mention of the Terai made my heart jump for joy. Lalmohan Babu's eyes were shining too. 'Let's see how it goes,' said Feluda non-committally. Thank goodness he didn't reject the idea outright. Mr Batra said 'Goodbye' and left.

'Why didn't you tell him about what we saw in that pig alley?' Lalmohan Babu asked curiously.

'Because,' Feluda replied, 'it is not my wont to divulge every detail of my investigation to all and sundry. And certainly not to someone I have met only briefly.'

'I see. I understand. Felu Babu, I have learnt,' said Jatayu, chastened.

On the way back to our room, we ran into Mr Bhowmik on the stairs. 'Can you recognize this?' he asked, holding up a medicine bottle. 'Benadryl Expectorant' said its label. It was a familiar enough sight—I was given the same red syrup at home every time I had a cough.

'Yes, I can certainly recognize the bottle, but the colour of the syrup seems a little different, doesn't it?' asked Feluda.

'Oh, can you see a difference in the colour? Then you are exceptionally observant. I noticed a difference in the smell.' He unscrewed the cap and offered the bottle to Feluda, who sniffed a couple of times and said, 'Yes, there is a subtle difference. You must have a very sensitive nose!'

'Yes, I do! And you know what I am going to do? I'll take this bottle right back to the chemist, and ask for my money back. I mean it. Didn't I tell you virtually every medicine these days is adulterated? Why, I've even heard they put chalk in baby food! Even innocent babies aren't going to be spared!'

We had told Mr Batra that Lalmohan Babu and I needed a car for the day. A Japanese Toyota arrived at nine. When we left a few minutes later, Feluda was poring over the telephone directory. 'Just noting down the addresses of the local chemists,' he said.

Only a place like Kathmandu could have both Swayambhunath, a Buddhist stupa and Pashupatinath, a Hindu temple.

With a brief 'Tapesh, you can look at the view', Lalmohan Babu disappeared inside the temple. When he came out, his forehead was smeared with sandalwood paste. He had clearly been blessed by the priest.

The temple was made chiefly of wood. Its doors and the spire were plated with gold and silver. The first thing one saw on coming through the main gate was a huge statue of Nandi, also covered in gold. A walk down a courtyard brought the River Bagmati into view. The mountains stood on the other side of the river.

The way to Swayambhu was through a road that wound up a hill like a snake. Our car stopped before a flight of stairs. We'd have to climb these and walk the rest of the way, we were told.

There were little stalls near the stairs, selling Tibetan goods. Lalmohan Babu suddenly seemed quite keen on buying a prayer wheel. It wasn't really a wheel—a small box was attached to one end of a stick. A chain hung from the box, with a little ball fixed at its tip. If one twirled the stick, the whole contraption moved round and round.

These prayer wheels were made of wood, copper, brass and ivory. Lalmohan Babu wanted a wooden one, but it turned out that it was too expensive. All prices had been fixed, no doubt, with rich American tourists in mind. With a sigh, Lalmohan Babu came away.

The stupa was built on top of the mountain two thousand years ago. What was most striking about it was a pillar that stood below it. Several pairs of eyes were painted on it, making it seem as though they had witnessed, for years and years, every event that occurred in the Kathmandu Valley, but every secret was safe with them. They would never speak out.

The flat open area on which the stupa stood was packed with people and monkeys. 'Damn these animals! One of them just poked me!' I heard Lalmohan Babu exclaim. We didn't, of course, know then that it wasn't a monkey. But I shall come to that later.

The real incident took place in Patan, which was on the other side of the Bagmati, three miles from Kathmandu. Our car had to pass through a huge gate to enter the town. We stopped at a shop to buy a couple of American Coca-Cola cans, and then made our way to the local Darbar Square. I will not go into lengthy descriptions of what we saw. Feluda, as a matter of fact, warned me not to get carried away. 'When you write about our adventure in Nepal,' he told me when we returned home, 'make sure it doesn't read like a tourist guide.'

Suffice it to say that the temples, stupas, palaces, exquisite wooden carvings and a statue of the king atop a golden pillar were so spectacular that Lalmohan

Babu kept breaking into exclamations every three minutes. 'Incredible!' he would say, 'Incomparable! Unbelievable! Inimitable! Fascinating! Unforgettable!' God knows how long he'd have continued if we were not distracted by a certain event.

We had left Darbar Square and turned right to find ourselves in yet another market called Mangal Bazar. It was full of handicrafts and other knick-knacks from both Nepal and Tibet. We went through the stalls, looking at their wares. Lalmohan Babu began inspecting prayer wheels once more. He picked up a few, but rejected them saying, 'The carving on these isn't good enough.' Things here were considerably cheaper than at Swayambhu.

About five minutes later, we noticed an old house where the market ended. A tempo was standing in front of it, being loaded with goods. This area was quiet, being some distance away from the hubbub of the main market.

As we got closer, we realized that what was being loaded on the tempo was nothing but what Lalmohan Babu had spent all day trying to buy—stacks and stacks of prayer wheels.

'This must be a factory,' Lalmohan Babu observed, looking at the house. 'I think this is where the stuff is made, and sent to Kathmandu. Which means . . . they might sell them cheaper here. Shall I go in and ask?'

'Yes, that's a good idea.'

But we were to be disappointed. The man supervising the loading shook his head and said, 'No, these are not for sale. These were made for a special order. You'll have to go back to the main market.'

'Oh no! Just my l—' Lalmohan Babu stopped abruptly, staring at a figure that was walking up the lane.

It was a Tibetan man. We recognized him instantly. He was still wearing the same yellow cap and the long red coat. One of his eyes was smaller than the other. This was our dozy old friend from the Tibetan shop in that pig alley. He stopped and went into the house through a side entrance. Or, at least, we couldn't see him any more. The door through which he appeared to have passed wasn't directly visible from where we were standing. If we took a few steps down the lane on the left, we might be able to see things better.

Suddenly, it became imperative to find out where that man had got to.

We turned into the lane on our left and proceeded to walk, as casually as we could. Only a few seconds later, we saw a door, made of solid wood and very delicately carved. It was locked from the inside. The Tibetan must have slipped in through this door and locked it behind him. But how could we be sure?

There was not a soul in sight. But someone was playing an instrument at the back of the house. We turned again to walk around the house. This time, we found its back door. It was much smaller in size, and had been left ajar. A Nepali beggar sat opposite the door, playing a sarinda. A rusted tin lay by his side. Our appearance did not disturb him at all. He continued to play a slow and rather mournful Nepali tune. His eyes were half-closed.

Lalmohan Babu dropped a few coins into the tin and asked under his breath, 'Shall we go in?'

'Yes, why not?'

'What if we're seen? What if someone asks us what we're doing inside?'

'Well, we can simply say we're tourists, and were curious to see the inside of an old house!'

'All right. Let's go.'

A quick look around showed that there was still no one about on the street. The beggar went on playing, unperturbed. We stepped in through the back door.

There was a passage. A portion of a courtyard could be seen where the passage ended. A strange, rhythmic noise came from beyond the courtyard. Were there rooms on the other side? We tiptoed our way down the passage.

Here was a door on our left. It opened at a slight touch. The room it led to was dark. Should we—?

Oh God, there were footsteps! Someone was coming from the opposite end. The sound of footsteps began to get louder. Very soon, we were going to be discovered. There was a sudden tightness in my throat. If this person coming down the passage asked us who we were, I knew I couldn't speak.

The beggar outside was now playing a different tune. It was a faster one and much more cheerful. But there was no time to think. I caught Lalmohan Babu's hand and pulled him into the dark room on our left, and quietly shut the door. The footsteps went past the door and out of the house.

The beggar had stopped playing. We could hear voices. Clearly, whoever just walked out of the house was talking to him.

I looked around helplessly. A shaft of light was coming in through a skylight. I could now spot a few things in the room. There was a string bed, a large copper bowl and a few clothes hanging from a rack. On my right was another door, leading to another room. An odd instinct made me slip into this second room, dragging Lalmohan Babu with me.

Pieces of wood and cardboard boxes filled the room. Besides these were a few statues, wooden frames and, lying in a corner, three prayer wheels. Behind this room was a veranda. The courtyard lay on the other side. That strange noise had stopped. A different noise now made my heart jump into my mouth. The footsteps were coming back. The man was obviously looking for us.

I heard him walk down the passage, then retrace his steps and stop outside the first room we had walked into. In a matter of seconds, he had walked across and opened the door of the room we were hiding in. I saw him cross the threshold and hesitate for a moment before his eyes fell on us.

The room being almost totally dark, I could not see his face at all. But I knew what I must do. Without another thought, I sprang up and attacked the man, trying to pin him against the wall. But I couldn't. He was much taller than I, and heavier. He shook me off, then grabbed me by the lapel of my jacket and picked me up straight off the floor. He would probably then have tossed me aside, but Lalmohan Babu stepped in at this point and caught his arms, trying to shake them free.

The man proved to be a good deal stronger than we had thought. With one mighty push of his elbow, he made Lalmohan Babu spin and fall on a pile of cardboard boxes. I placed my own hands under his chin and tilted his head back as far as I could. But I could sense it wasn't really going to make much difference for the man was still holding me high, and would, any minute—

Clang!

Suddenly, the hands holding me went limp. I dropped to my feet, on solid ground.

Our adversary was lying on the floor, knocked unconscious by a blow on his head. Lalmohan Babu was standing by my side, staring dumbly at the wooden prayer wheel he was still holding in his hand.

Ten seconds later, we were out on the street, walking as fast as our feet would take us.

The prayer wheel was resting peacefully in Lalmohan Babu's bag.

CHAPTER 8

Before coming to Nepal, Feluda and I had often talked about our past adventures and wondered what had become of those villains Feluda had exposed. Bonobihari Sarkar of Lucknow, Mandar Bose in Jaisalmer, Mr Gore of Bombay, Maganlal Meghraj of Benaras—had they been adequately punished and had they learnt their lesson? Or were they still out there somewhere, spinning more webs of crime? After all, they all had enormous cunning. Why, some of them had so nearly managed to get away!

Little did we know that here in Kathmandu we were going to find one of these figures so unexpectedly.

When we returned from Patan in the late afternoon, after having stopped for lunch at a restaurant (sadly for Lalmohan Babu, their menu did not include mo-mo), Feluda was lying on his bed, reading a book called

Black Market Medicine. One look at us made him raise an eyebrow.

'What's the matter with you? Where have you been?' he asked.

We told him. Feluda heard us out, throwing in a few rapid questions every now and then, and added, 'Well done!'

It was nice to be praised, but I knew what we had done was a big step for all of us. Something fishy was going on in that house. I had no doubt about that.

'If I could, I would give you a special reward for bravery,' Feluda went on, 'but let's have a look at your weapon, Lalmohan Babu!'

Lalmohan Babu took out the prayer wheel from his shoulder bag.

'Have you checked if it's got the prayer in it?'

'Prayer? What prayer?'

'*Om Manipadmey Hoom.* It's a Tibetan prayer. These words are either written or printed a thousand times on a piece of paper, which is then placed inside the wheel.'

'Really? How would they put it in?'

The top of that little box with the chain should unscrew like a cap. You should find a piece of paper in it.'

Lalmohan Babu twisted the top of the box. It came off quite easily. He peered inside and said, 'No, sir, no sign of a prayer.'

'Nothing at all?'

Lalmohan Babu moved closer to the window where the light was better and looked again. 'No—wait a minute! There is something. It's glistening in the light.'

'Let's see.'

Feluda took the prayer wheel from Lalmohan Babu and had a good look into the box, holding it under a table lamp. Then he turned it over. A few pieces of glass slipped out.

'Look at that large piece, Feluda. It must have been a glass pipe or something.'

'No, not a glass pipe. It was an ampoule. Someone must have broken it accidentally, so they cast the whole thing aside.'

'Does that mean these prayer wheels are used to despatch spurious medicines?'

'Yes, that is entirely likely. What they probably do is fill these wheels with ampoules or capsules, and store them in packing cases in that house in the pig alley. From there they go to wholesalers, who pass them on to pharmacies and chemists. Tell me, did the packing cases you saw today being loaded on the tempo look like the ones we saw in that other house?'

'Identical,' Lalmohan Babu replied.

'I see,' Feluda frowned. 'The second Mr Batra must be in charge of supplies. And if they're operating on a large scale, they're probably sending some of this stuff across to India. God knows how many people in UP and Bihar are being treated with these spurious drugs. Even if someone suspects something, they won't do anything about it. We've grown so accustomed to turning a blind eye to all malpractices!'

Feluda rose from the bed and began pacing restlessly. Lalmohan Babu sat twirling the prayer wheel. So far, he had nearly always been just an onlooker in all our adventures. Today, he was out on the stage himself. I looked at my watch. It was nearly 4 p.m.

'Lalmohan Babu,' I said, 'isn't it time to go and collect your trousers?'

'Hey, that's right! I had forgotten all about them.' He sprang to his feet, adding, 'We are going to the casino tonight, aren't we? I'm getting the trousers made solely for that purpose, you see.'

Feluda stopped pacing. Then he shook his head vigorously, as if to drive away all unpleasant thoughts, and said, 'Good idea! Today we have earned ourselves a visit to the casino. Yes, we'll spend an hour there after dinner.'

We left at 8.30, in a bus arranged by our hotel.

It soon became clear that the casino was away from the main city. We drove for about fifteen minutes before our bus went up a hill, passed through a gate, drove past a lawn and a swimming pool and finally stopped at the entrance to the casino. Feluda had already told us that the casino was part of a large hotel. When we got out of the bus, I realized that the casino stood separately; one didn't actually have to go into the main hotel to get to it.

Lalmohan Babu seemed determined to behave exactly the way he had seen people behave in Western films. He was dressed for the part too. New trousers made here in Kathmandu, a light green jerkin from New Market in Calcutta, and a Nepali cap added a certain polish to his appearance.

He strode in, saying 'Hel-lo!' to the two gentlemen who sat near the entrance to check the five-dollar card our hotel had given us. They looked up, startled. But by then Lalmohan Babu had walked on, studying his card carefully. A few seconds later, he nearly ran into a Japanese lady who was coming up a flight of stairs. He skipped aside just in time, with a brilliant smile and a 'Hex-hex-cuse me-hee!' I had to look away quickly to stop myself from laughing. Inside the main casino, however, his confident air vanished. I caught him looking at Feluda appealingly.

'Take another look at your card,' said Feluda. 'You'll find five coupons for five different games. I suggest you first try your hand at jackpot, it's the simplest. If you tear off one of those coupons and hand it in at that counter, they'll give you the equivalent of one dollar in Nepali rupees. I think you'll get about eleven rupees. That means you get eleven chances at the jackpot. If you run out of money but still wish to go on, you'll have to pay out of your own pocket. I don't need to remind you of what happens to people who don't know when to stop. Just think of Yudhishthir in the Mahabharata!'

After collecting our money from the counter, Lalmohan Babu and I made our way to the nearest jackpot machine. Feluda walked into the next room, which was bigger and had roulette, pontoon and blackjack as well as jackpot.

'It's all quite simple, really,' I said to Lalmohan Babu. 'Look, here's a slot machine. All you need to do is put a coin into this slot, just as you'd do in a weighing machine, and pull this handle on the right. The machine will do the rest.'

'What does that mean?'

'If you win, more coins will come out of the machine. If you lose, then obviously nothing happens. The machine just swallows your money.'

'I see. Shall I—?'

'Yes, go on!'

'Ah well, here goes . . .!'

A whirring noise told us the money had gone to the right place. A light came on instantly and a sign said, 'Coin accepted'.

'All right. Now pull this handle. Pull it hard.'

Lalmohan Babu yanked with all his might. Behind a small square window on the machine were three pictures: a yellow fruit, a red fruit and a bell. As the handle was turned, the machine began whirring again and the pictures started to change. Five seconds later, they stopped with a click and showed a different combination—two yellow fruits and a blue flower.

In the next instant, two coins slipped out of the machine. Look, look!' Lalmohan Babu cried. Does that mean I won?'

'Yes, certainly. You've now got two rupees. If you're lucky enough, you might insert a rupee and get a hundred in return. Here's a chart that tells you how much each combination will fetch. All right?'

'Ok-kay!'

I found another machine for myself. There were at least another ten machines in this smaller room. A man was sitting in a corner with small plastic bowls which could be used to keep our coins in. I got two from him and gave one to Lalmohan Babu.

Very soon, we were both totally engrossed in our game. I lost all track of time. All that seemed to matter was pulling the handle of the machines and then waiting with bated breath. This must be my lucky day, I thought, watching the little bowl fill with coins. Despite Feluda's warning, I wanted to go on playing. Out of the corner of my eye, I saw Lalmohan Babu walk over to the counter and change his coins for bank notes. He was winning too.

At this moment, however, Feluda turned up, accompanied by a young lady.

'We'll take a break,' he said, the perfect spoilsport.

'Why, sir?' asked Lalmohan Babu, annoyed at being interrupted.

'We're wanted in 433.'

'What?'

The young lady explained quickly, 'A friend of yours is staying here in room 433. He's sent a special request for you to go and meet him.'

'Who is this friend?' Lalmohan Babu was still looking cross.

'He didn't tell me his name, but said you knew him very well.'

'Let's go and meet him,' said Feluda. 'I feel quite curious. Besides, we can come back here in ten minutes.'

Rather reluctantly, Lalmohan Babu and I turned to go. The lady came with us up to the lift, then said 'namaskar' and left. She must have been an employee of the hotel.

Room 433 turned out to be the last room at the end of a long corridor. Feluda rang the bell. 'Come in!'

said a gruff voice. The door had been left unlocked. Feluda pushed it open and went in. Lalmohan Babu and I followed.

Only one lamp was on in the huge living room. Someone was sitting on a sofa at the far end, but we couldn't see his face clearly as the lamp was directly behind him. Opposite him was a video showing some American film. After a few seconds of silence, the man spoke. 'Come in, Mr Mitter!' he said. 'Come on in, Uncle!'

My head began to reel, and my knees suddenly turned to jelly.

I knew this voice well. We all did. It belonged to a man we had met in the holiest of holy places—Varanasi; and Feluda had freely admitted that this man had been the toughest among all the criminals he had ever had to deal with.

Maganlal Meghraj.

What was this dangerous crook doing in Kathmandu?

CHAPTER 9

'**D**o sit down,' Maganlal invited, switching the video off. Lalmohan Babu and I sat down on a settee, Feluda took a chair.

'Well, Mr Mitter?'

Feluda said nothing. Like me, he was looking straight at Maganlal. He hadn't changed much in these few years. He was still wearing a dhoti and a sherwani. The latter had clearly been made by an expert tailor. What had changed, of course, were his surroundings. A dark and dingy house in a narrow alley in Varanasi was a far cry indeed from this luxurious suite in a five-star hotel.

'This time, I hope, you are on a real holiday, Mr Mitter?' Maganlal asked.

'No, Maganlalji, not really,' Feluda said pleasantly. 'Some people are just not destined to have a holiday without having to mix business with pleasure. I am one of them.'

'What business have you got here, Mr Mitter?' Maganlal picked up a telephone. 'Tea or coffee? You can get the best-quality Darjeeling tea here.'

'In that case, let's have tea.'

Maganlal rang room service, ordered tea for all of us, and turned to Feluda again. 'You are a big hero in India, Mr Mitter. But Nepal is a foreign country. Do you know many people here?'

'Well, I seem to have found at least one person I know!'

Maganlal smiled wryly. His eyes did not move from Feluda's face.

'Are you surprised to find me here?'

'Yes, I am, a little.' Feluda lit a Charminar. 'Not to find you outside the prison—I realize you have all the right connections to have organized an early release— but to see you outside Benaras.'

'Why? Benaras is a holy place, and so is Kathmandu. We have Baba Vishwanath there, and here's Pashupatinath. My karma, you see, is related to places of dharma! What do you say, Uncle?'

'He heh!' Lalmohan Babu tried to laugh. I could see he had gone visibly pale. All the horrors of Arjun's knife-throwing must have come rushing back.

'You talk of your karma, Maganlalji,' said Feluda casually. 'Would that by any chance involve drugs and medicines?'

A cold shiver ran down my spine. How could Feluda be so reckless?

'Drugs? Medicines? What are you talking about?' Maganlal sounded perfectly taken aback.

'If you have nothing to do with them, then do you mind telling me what you're doing here?'

'No, not at all. But we must have a fair exchange.'

'All right. You go first.'

'It's all very simple, Mr Mitter. I am an art dealer— you know I like statues and paintings, don't you? Many houses in Nepal are crammed with such stuff. My job is to collect them.'

Feluda remained silent. I could hear Lalmohan Babu breathing heavily.

'Now, you tell me about yourself.'

'I don't think you've been entirely honest with me,' Feluda replied, 'but I am going to be quite frank. I am here to investigate a murder.'

'Murder?'

'Yes'

'You mean the murder of Mr Som?'

I gaped, Lalmohan Babu drew in his breath sharply. Only Feluda's face remained expressionless. Yes, that's right, Maganlalji,' he said coolly. 'Mr Anikendra Som.'

A waiter came in with the tea. He placed the tray on a table in front of Maganlal.

'It is my belief,' Feluda continued when the waiter had gone, 'that Mr Som had started to cause some concern to a certain individual. So he had to be removed from the scene.'

Maganlal began pouring. 'One or two?' he asked me, holding the sugar pot. It was filled with sugar cubes.

'One, please,' I replied. Maganlal dropped a cube in my cup and passed it to me. Then he turned to Lalmohan Babu, who was eyeing the cubes with open suspicion. I knew he was thinking of hippies and LSD.

'What about you, Uncle? Two? Three?'

'N-no, no.'

'No sugar at all?'

'No, th-thank you.'

I looked at him in surprise. We all knew he had a sweet tooth.

'You amaze me, Uncle,' Maganlal said with a slight smile. 'Why are you saying no?'

This time, Lalmohan Babu gave me a sidelong glance and said, 'OK. One, please.' Perhaps the fact that I had accepted a cube gave him courage. Feluda too was given one. He went on speaking, 'I think Mr Som had unearthed an illegal racket. He had gone to Calcutta to make further inquiries, and to meet me. He was killed before he could do so. Since you appear to know about the murder, naturally one would wish to know if you are involved in any way in this case.'

Maganlal stared at Feluda for a few moments, his eyes narrowed, his lips contorted in a twisted smile. Lalmohan Babu and I sipped our tea. It really was the very best Darjeeling tea anyone could get.

'Jagdeesh!' Maganlal shouted suddenly. I couldn't help but start. A door behind Maganlal opened and a man came into the room silently. Lalmohan Babu put his cup down on the table with a clatter.

The man called Jagdeesh standing behind Maganlal was the second Mr Batra. There were very slight differences in his appearance which were apparent only because we could watch him, for the first time, at close quarters. His eyes were lighter than our Mr Batra's, his hair was greyer, and—most important of all—the look in his eyes held not even a glimmer of warmth.

'Do you know this man?' asked Maganlal.

'We haven't met him, but we know him by sight.'

'Then listen carefully, Mr Private Investigator. Do not harass Jagdeesh. I know you have been trying to track him down ever since you arrived. I will not tolerate your interference, Mr Mitter. Jagdeesh is my right-hand man.'

'Even though he is left-handed?'

Feluda was still speaking lightly. Before Maganlal could say anything, he asked another question. 'Are you aware that there is a gentleman who looks almost exactly like your Jagdeesh?'

Maganlal frowned darkly. 'Yes, Mr Mitter. I know that. If this other man is a friend of yours, tell him to take care. He must think before he acts. You have seen the cremation ground near the temple of Pashupatinath, haven't you, Uncle? You went there today, didn't you?' Without a word, Lalmohan Babu finished his tea in one long gulp and replaced the cup carefully on the table. His hand trembled slightly.

'If Batra thinks he can commit a crime and try to get Jagdeesh blamed for it, then within two days Batra's body will be cremated in that ground. Go tell your friend, Mr Mitter!'

'Very well, I shall pass on your message.'

Feluda too finished his tea and rose. 'We must take our leave now, Maganlalji. Thank you for the tea. It really was very good.'

Maganlal made no comment. Nor did he move from his seat. He simply reached for the remote control and switched the video on again.

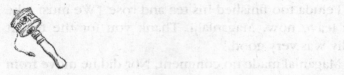

CHAPTER 10

We returned to our hotel soon after our meeting with Maganlal. None of us had any idea that there was more in store.

We found Harinath Chakravarty waiting for us in the lounge. This surprised us all. What was he doing here so late at night? It was past eleven.

'Let's go up to our room,' Feluda said. Harinath Babu joined us without a word. He was clearly anxious about something.

'What is the matter, Mr Chakravarty?' asked Feluda when we were all seated in our room.

Harinath Babu took a few seconds to collect his thoughts. Then he said slowly, 'When Himadri left us so suddenly, I couldn't think straight. Besides, it didn't seem worthwhile to talk about such matters when nothing would bring him back.'

'What are you talking about?'

'About three years ago,' Harinath Babu replied after a pause, 'Himadri had exposed a gang who were smuggling things like ganja and charas. I told you, didn't I, that he often took his helicopter both to the north and south of Nepal? He discovered the den of these smugglers in the north and informed the police. The whole gang was caught.'

'Are you telling us, that just before his death, he had come upon something involving another gang?'

'He didn't tell me anything. But a few days before he died, I saw him discuss something rather animatedly with his friend. I told him not to meddle in these things. These criminals can be totally merciless. But he only laughed and told me not to worry. I believe, Mr Mitter, my son would have died anyway. If an attack of tetanus did not kill him, these crooks would have taken his life somehow.'

'Why are you saying this?'

Harinath Babu took out a piece of paper and handed it to Feluda. It had something scribbled on it in red ink.

'We found this in his trouser pocket after he died.'

'Is it written in Nepali?'

'Yes. It says, "You have gone too far."'

Feluda returned the piece of paper to Harinath Babu and smiled wryly.

'The biggest irony is that one who was on the verge of exposing a drug racket had to die of a spurious drug himself.'

'Do you really believe the injection he was given wasn't genuine?' Harinath Babu asked.

'Yes. Hopefully, by tomorrow, we shall know for sure. You see, I've asked Dr Divakar to have a sample analysed.'

'I see. Well, that is all I came to tell you. I hope it helps in some way,' said Harinath Babu and stood up.

'It certainly does. I am now much clearer in my mind about what I'm looking for. Thank you, Mr Chakravarty.'

Harinath Babu left. Lalmohan Babu too said 'Goodnight' and went to his room.

I went straight to bed after this. What a day it had been!

I must have fallen asleep immediately, but was woken a little later by the doorbell. A quick glance at my watch told me it was a quarter past twelve. Who on earth could it be at this hour? I got out of bed and opened the door. Then my mouth fell open.

It was Lalmohan Babu. In his left hand he held a scrap of paper. In his right was the prayer wheel. His lips were parted in a smile that could only be described as beatific.

'Hoom! Hoom! Hoom!' he said, coming into the room, turning the prayer wheel. I took the piece of paper from his hand and saw what was written on it in English. 'You have been warned,' it said. It was written with the same red ink as the warning in Nepali we had just seen.

Feluda was sitting up on his bed. I passed the paper on to him and asked Lalmohan Babu, 'Where did you find it?'

He patted the right pocket of his jacket. He had been wearing the same jacket in the morning. I remembered him saying a monkey had pulled at his clothes.

'Om-m-m-m!' said Lalmohan Babu, sitting down on a chair. The smile hadn't left his face. I looked at Feluda. He was staring at Lalmohan Babu, looking concerned. 'LSD,' he whispered as he caught my eye.

That sugar cube!

Maganlal had made tea for all of us. Since Feluda and I were still sane, he had obviously tampered only with Lalmohan Babu's tea, just to make a fool of him. What a swine he was!

Lalmohan Babu had stopped smiling. For some unknown reason, he was now looking decidedly displeased. 'Take off your skull!' he said sternly to Feluda. 'I said take it off, you old scallywag!'

'Maganlal—you scoundrel!' said Feluda under his breath.

Lalmohan Babu turned his eyes to the glass of water on the bedside table, and frowned. Then, slowly, his eyes widened in amazement and he began smiling again.

'Ooooh!' he said appreciatively. 'Just look at those colours! Vibgyor! Look, Tapesh, have you ever seen such shades, such hues?'

Vibgyor? Could he actually see a rainbow in that glass of water?

'It's vibrating! Have you ever seen colour vibrate?'

Then he fell silent. I began to feel sleepy again and nodded off. But I woke with a start almost instantly as I heard him shout, 'Mice!'

He was sitting ramrod straight, staring at the floor.

'Mice!' he said again. 'Terramyce, tetramyce, subamyce, chloromyce . . . compromise . . . there they

are, wriggling on the floor . . . don't play the fool with
me, I tell you!'

He jumped up and began stamping his foot on the
carpet, as if that was the only way he could get rid of
the mice. Then he began hopping all over the room,
still stamping his foot constantly. I hoped fervently the
room below ours was empty.

'Finished! Ah, at last! All ticks finished!'

He sat down again. How had the mice turned into
ticks?

'Antibioticks! Killed them all, I did. Ha!'

Now his eyes drooped. Perhaps the sudden burst of
activity had tired him out. Om-m-m-m!' he said softly,
looking very pleased with himself. 'Om-m-m-m-mo-mo-
mo!'

I couldn't keep my eyes open any longer. When I
opened them, sunlight was streaming in through an
open window. Feluda had already had his bath, shaved
and seemed ready to go out. He finished talking to
someone on the phone and replaced the receiver when
he saw I was awake.

'Get up, Topshe, we have lots to do. Mr Batra must
be told he's not as safe as we had thought.'

'Whom were you calling?'

'The police. They gave me some good news. The
two governments have agreed to carry out a joint
investigation.'

'That's splendid!'

'Yes. But I made another call, and that worried me.'

'What happened?'

'I rang Dr Divakar. Apparently, he received an urgent call early this morning and left. I don't like this at all.'

'Why?'

'I have a feeling the gang we're after found out I had asked him to get a sample tested. But I could be wrong. I'll call him again a little later. If I can't get him on the phone, I'll go straight to his dispensary.'

'Er . . . where is Lalmohan Babu?'

'He left an hour ago, looking as though he had attained moksha. But he was quite calm, no problem there. The whole effect of the drug will take about eight hours to wear off.'

'Were you up all night?'

'Yes, someone had to keep an eye on him.'

'Is he normal now?'

'Almost. Just before going he told me one-third of my brain was made of solid stuff, the remainder was water. God knows what he meant.'

CHAPTER 11

It took me half an hour to get ready. Feluda had already gone down. I found him waiting for me by the reception, pacing anxiously.

'Dr Divakar hasn't returned to his house,' he told me. 'I rang him again. His family doesn't know where he's gone.'

'And Batra?'

'I couldn't get through. I'll try once more, then I'll go over to his office. We need a car, anyway.'

Lalmohan Babu came down in less than five minutes, looking absolutely normal. But a few things he said implied the effects of LSD hadn't quite worn off. There was a large Nepali mask hanging on the wall near the reception. He stroked it gently and asked, 'What is the name of the palace in England?'

'Buckingham Palace?'

'Yes, but it's nothing compared to this.'

'Compared to what?'

'This hotel. Hotel Lumumba.'

'Lumbini.'

'All right. Lumbini. He was born here, wasn't he?'

'Who?'

'Gautam Buddha.'

'Not in this hotel!'

'Why, you mean to say they didn't have hotels before Christ?'

Luckily, this weird conversation could not continue for long, for Feluda turned up soon after and said we had to finish our breakfast quickly and go to Sun Travels, for he still couldn't get them on the phone.

We decided to have just a cup of coffee for breakfast. Something told me today was going to be another eventful day.

It took us only five minutes to walk down to Sun Travels. Their office was obviously new, and very smartly furnished. Mr Pradhan, Batra's secretary, ushered us into Batra's room; and then dropped a bombshell.

'Mr Batra has gone out, I'm afraid,' he said. 'A very important person rang him this morning, you see. He wanted to see our new bungalow in the Rapti Valley. So Mr Batra had to go with him. But he did tell me you might need a car. I can arrange one quite easily.'

'Thank you. But could you please tell us who this important person was?'

'Certainly. It was Mr Meghraj. He's staying at the Oberoi. A very important art dealer.'

Lalmohan Babu clutched my hand. The very mention of Meghraj's name had brought him to his senses. But Mr Batra? Who could have known he would fall into Maganlal's trap so soon?

'How long does it take to get to your bungalow?' Feluda asked.

'You will need to go via Hetaora—that's 150 km. You might wish to stop for lunch in Hetaora. Our bungalow is new, you see, so the kitchen isn't ready yet. Turn right as you come out of Hetaora and go along the river for three kilometres. You'll find our bungalow there, in the middle of the jungle. It's a beautiful spot.'

'I see. Could you have a car pick us up from the hotel in half an hour?'

'Very well, sir. No problem!'

'You two go back to the hotel and wait for me. I have to go to Darbar Square. I won't be long,' Feluda said as we came out of Sun Travels.

The car arrived in twenty minutes. Feluda took twenty-five. 'Had to go to Freak Street,' he explained.

'Where is that?'

'Not very far. That's where most hippies stay.'

In five minutes, we were on our way to Hetaora. Feluda had his notebook open and was studying its entries, frowning deeply. Lalmohan Babu had been restored to his normal self, although I noticed he had a strangely tranquil air, suggesting he was totally at peace with the world. Looking at the scenery, he made only one comment: 'I had double vision yesterday. Now I can see only one of everything.'

Feluda looked up at this and said with a slightly preoccupied air, 'That is true. But then, so is its reverse.'

I found this remark extremely mystifying.

We had climbed four thousand feet from Kathmandu. Snow-capped peaks were clearly in view. Soon, it became necessary to take out woollen mufflers, and drink the hot coffee we had brought in a flask.

Half an hour later, we began climbing down, making our way to the Shivalik Hills. The Rapti Valley and the town of Hetaora were not far.

'Topshe, do you know Batra's first name?' Feluda asked suddenly, closing his notebook.

'No. He never told us, did he?'

'He didn't. But you should have noticed the nameplate on his desk. It's Anantlal Batra.'

When we reached Hetaora, it was nearly 2 p.m. None of us felt hungry, so we didn't stop for lunch. 'What is food at a moment like this?' asked Lalmohan Babu. It is nothing!'

The driver drove on, turning right from the highway. I could now see the River Rapti gushing through the trees. The road we were on was lined with tall trees on both sides. I couldn't get over the fact that we were actually passing through the famous Terai, which was well known for its vicious wild animals. I had read such a lot about it! After the Sepoy Mutiny in 1857, Nana Saheb was supposed to have taken refuge in its leafy depths, together with all his men.

We took another right turn, which brought us to a dirt road. A few minutes later, we saw the bungalow. A large area had been cleared to build it. It had a sizeable compound. Our car passed through the gate and went up a cobbled driveway. Then it stopped just before the front door.

I realized how quiet the place was as soon as our driver switched off the engine. He then got out and moved towards the garage. I could see another car parked there. We too got out of the car and went into the house. The front door was open.

'Come in, Mr Mitter!'

It wasn't difficult to recognize the deep voice of Maganlal Meghraj. We walked into the living room. There were two settees. The floor was covered by a Tibetan carpet. A radio stood on a small table on one side, and on a shelf were a few books and magazines.

Maganlal was sitting on one of the settees, eating puri-sabzi from a tiffin carrier. A servant stood waiting with a towel and a bowl of water. There was no one else in the room.

'I knew you'd come,' he said, wiping his hands. By this time, we were all seated. 'I also know why you've come,' Maganlal went on, 'but I am going to win this round. You can't have it your way each time, can you?' Feluda did not speak.

'I haven't forgotten the humiliation you caused me in Benaras, Mr Mitter. I am going to pay you back.'

I could hear a funny thudding noise coming from one of the rooms to our right. God knows what was causing it.

'Where is Mr Batra?' asked Feluda calmly, ignoring Maganlal's threat.

Maganlal clicked his tongue. 'Very sorry, Mr Mitter. I told you Jagdeesh was my right hand. One needs only one right hand, doesn't one? I saw no reason to have two.'

'You did not answer my question. Where is he?'

Batra is still alive. He'll be safe during the day. But who knows what might happen at night? There is a law against destroying wildlife. But tell me, have you ever heard of a law protecting a man from hungry wild animals?'

'Why did you leave Kathmandu, Maganlalji? Do you know what's happening there today?'

'You tell me.'

'Your factory in Patan and warehouse in Kathmandu are both being ransacked by the police.'

Maganlal burst into laughter. His massive body swayed from side to side. 'What kind of a fool do you take me for, Mr Mitter? The police will find nothing, absolutely nothing! The warehouse in the pig alley is empty, and all that is now being made in Patan are handicrafts. Perfectly genuine handicrafts. I have brought all my stuff with me, Mr Mitter. Didn't you see lorries going to India through Hetaora? They carry timber; and some of them, Mr Mitter, carry what I wish to have hidden in the timber. Yes, that is how I send fake drugs to India. Mind you, most of my work is done in India by Indians. Labels, capsules, ampoules, phials— they all come from India. The rest is done here, for Nepalis work harder— and better—than Indians.'

Maganlal stopped. I could hear crickets outside, making a racket. But what was that noise—?

Jagdeesh lifted a colourful embroidered curtain and came in, a revolver in his left hand. He stood mutely, pointing it at Feluda.

'Get up!' Maganlal ordered. We rose slowly.

'Raise your hands.' We did.

'Ganga! Kesri!'

Two other men came in and began to search us. One of them found Feluda's revolver and handed it to Maganlal.

The thudding noise seemed to have grown louder and more insistent. Maganlal looked faintly annoyed and said, 'I am sorry, Mr Mitter, but I had to get hold of another friend of yours. He was trying to get our drugs analysed and create more problems for us. So naturally he had to be stopped.'

'Will you feed him to the animals too?'

'No, no, Mr Mitter.' Maganlal grinned. 'I can use him to my own advantage. It's very useful to have a doctor to turn to. My heart—'

Before he could finish speaking, a number of things happened all at once. The two men called Ganga and Kesri had left the room. Now they came back carrying thick ropes. At this moment, a car drew up outside. Jagdeesh promptly removed the safety catch of his revolver; but Feluda was too quick for him. He leapt up in the air and kicked the revolver out of Jagdeesh's hand. But somehow the gun went off. A bullet shot out and hit the ceiling fan, making it spin.

In these few seconds, as if by magic, a large number of men had appeared out of nowhere. I couldn't recognize any of them, but could tell that they were all policemen in plain clothes from both India and Nepal. One of them grabbed Jagdeesh and pinned him against the wall.

Maganlal was on his feet, glaring with smouldering eyes. 'Don't touch me! Don't you dare!' he hissed.

'We'll deal with you in a minute, Maganlalji,' Feluda said, 'but first, let me get something settled.' He turned to Jagdeesh. 'I couldn't see your fingers properly because you were holding that gun,' said Feluda, 'but now . . . yes, I can see that two of your fingers have got ink on them. Are you still using that same old pen that leaks, Mr Batra?'

'Shut up, Mr Mitter!' shouted Maganlal. 'Just shut up! Jagdeesh is my—'

'Not Jagdeesh. Batra—Anantlal Batra—is your right hand. There is no Jagdeesh; nor is there a second Mr Batra. It's the same man. I'm sure the police can make him remove his contact lenses. There is something he doesn't yet know. His house was searched this morning after he left. The police found a lot of counterfeit money, which—no doubt—used to be produced in your factory in Patan.'

An officer from the Nepal Police brought out a large bundle of hundred-rupee notes. Batra went white.

'You made one false move in Calcutta, Mr Batra,' Feluda told him. In trying to establish that there were two Batras, you bought a kukri at the gift shop in your hotel and gave them a fake note. But you could not take it back, since later you had to pretend to be totally innocent. So the shop passed it on to the police. The number on it was the same as the number on all the notes they found in your house.'

Batra looked as though he wanted to sink through the floor. But Maganlal had not given up.

'I warn you, Mr Mitter—' he began.

'You're talking too much!' Feluda interrupted him. 'I must do something to keep you quiet. Topshe, get the man!'

I was quite willing to do this, but noticed, to my surprise, that Lalmohan Babu seemed much more keen to grab Maganlal and push him down on the sofa. He wriggled a lot, but the two of us held him back.

Feluda, in the meantime, had taken out two objects from his pocket. One of them was a sugar cube. This explained why he had gone to Freak Street. He forced it into Maganlal's mouth and made him swallow it.

The second object was a roll of cellotape. Feluda tore a portion of it and sealed Maganlal's mouth with it.

Finally, he put his hand inside his jacket pocket and brought out something that looked like a cigarette case. He handed it to one of the police officers and said, 'I had switched on this mini cassette recorder the minute we stepped into this room. You will get a lot of information from it, given by Mr Meghraj himself.'

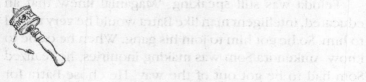

CHAPTER 12

'I believe Batra came into contact with Maganlal through his job as a PRO,' said Feluda.

We were sitting at a restaurant, on our way back to Kathmandu, having coffee and sandwiches. With us were Dr Divakar, Inspector Sharma of the Nepal Police and Inspector Joardar from Calcutta. We had found Dr Divakar in one of the rooms in the bungalow. His hands and feet were tied, and he had been gagged. But that had not stopped him from stamping his feet, making that thudding noise we had heard.

According to what Dr Divakar told the police this morning, Batra had called at his house and picked him up, saying there was an emergency case needing his attention. He had then collected Maganlal and the two men had forced him to go to the bungalow with them.

Maganlal and his men were now back in Kathmandu, all under arrest. I was dying to know how he'd react to the LSD, but knew I'd have to wait until tomorrow to find out.

Feluda was still speaking. 'Maganlal knew that an educated, intelligent man like Batra would be very useful to him. So he got him to join his gang. When he came to know Anikendra Som was making inquiries, he realized Som had to be got out of the way. He chose Batra for this task. Batra took the same plane from Kathmandu as Som, and managed to get talking with him, although he later denied this. We found one sentence in Mr Som's notebook that said, "Find out about AB." I had thought at first that meant antibiotics, but the minute I learnt Batra's first name was Anantlal, I realized Som was referring to him. It could be that something Batra said made him suspicious.'

Feluda paused to take a sip from his cup, and continued, 'It now looks as though Mr Som had mentioned to Batra that he was going to meet me. Batra knew who I was. So he could guess that should Som get killed, I would be asked to make an investigation. He didn't know then that we would run into each other purely by accident. But when we did, the idea of creating a "double" occurred to him immediately. I have to admit it was a very clever idea. He happened to have bought a blue shirt just before he met me, which, in fact, he was still carrying in a plastic bag. Soon after we parted, he must have gone into a shop for readymade garments and changed into the blue shirt in one of their fitting rooms. Then he deliberately walked past us, pretending never to have seen me in his life.

The next day, he staged a little drama in the gift shop, and came to my house in the evening to convince me of the existence of this "double". The day after that, he left his hotel very early in the morning in a taxi, went to Mr Som's hotel at five and killed him. Then he went to the airport and caught his flight to Kathmandu at nine o'clock. He left the kukri behind to make me think that the murderer was the "fake" Mr Batra.'

'When did you first begin to have doubts?' asked Inspector Joardar.

'Well, you see, when I first met him, he got me to write down my address in his notebook. This was necessary, since he would have had to use his left hand if he wrote it himself. Now, that would have spoilt things, for he was then trying to establish that it was the other Batra who was left-handed. But I noticed something odd about the nib of his fountain pen. If a left-handed person uses a fountain pen, he holds it at a certain angle and the nib gets worn. A right-handed person then finds it difficult to write with the same pen. I felt the same difficulty, but paid no attention at the time. When I saw that the murderer of Mr Som was left-handed, my suspicions were roused and I felt I should probe into the matter a bit further in Kathmandu. But I did not know then that it was a case of two murders, not one.'

'Two murders?' Lalmohan Babu couldn't hide his amazement. We all stared. Which was the second murder? What was Feluda talking about?

But Feluda said nothing. Finally, Dr Divakar broke the silence.

'He's right,' he said. 'I did get a sample of anti-tetanus serum from my dispensary and had it tested. It turned out to be just plain water. I was going to call on Mr Mitter and tell him personally, but I never got the chance. Those who deal with spurious drugs certainly deserve to be called murderers. I agree with Mr Mitter.'

'But, Dr Divakar, I am not talking of spurious drugs,' said Feluda.

This time, even the doctor looked startled. 'Then what are you talking about?' he asked.

'I'll explain that in a minute. Before that I wish to mention something else. Three years ago, Himadri Chakravarty had exposed a gang of criminals. His father told us he was working on catching another group meddling with medicines and drugs. If he succeeded, Maganlal and his men would have been in deep trouble. So obviously Maganlal had a strong motive for getting him out of the way.'

'But how?'

'That was fairly simple. Maganlal got a doctor to help him.'

'A doctor?' Dr Divakar frowned.

'Yes.'

'Who? Which doctor do you mean?'

'A doctor who has suddenly come into a lot of money. He's now got a new house and a new car. He wears an expensive watch, glasses with golden frames . . .'

'What utter nonsense are you—?'

'—A doctor who looks at a mere scratch and gives an anti-tetanus shot, although he knows it is totally unnecessary. Do you think, Dr Divakar, that I didn't see through your clever ploy? All that business of getting yourself tied up and gagged was just an act, wasn't it? You are a member of Maganlal's team, aren't you? Just like Batra?'

Dr Divakar was actually trembling with rage. How is it possible, Mr Mitter, to kill with plain water?' he shouted.

'Not plain water, doctor. But it is easy enough to kill with poison. You used strychnine, didn't you? The symptoms Himadri showed once the injection had been given were very similar to symptoms of tetanus. Inspector Joardar, am I right?'

The inspector nodded gravely.

'Yes' he said, 'strychnine causes convulsions and other symptoms not very different from tetanus.'

Dr Divakar had risen to his feet. The inspector's words made him sink back into the chair, then roll off it and slip to the floor, his face hidden in his hands.

Our story ended here. But three things happened later which I ought to add.

One—the sugar cube Maganlal was made to swallow caused him much discomfort. He was reported to have scratched the walls of his cell like a cat for three hours continuously. Then he mistook a floorcloth for a plate of rubri, and chewed it to shreds.

Two—Feluda was given a cash reward by the Government of Nepal for unearthing not just those who were producing spurious drugs, but also those involved in making counterfeit money. The amount given was not insubstantial—we had a fair bit left over even after meeting all our expenses.

Three—Lalmohan Babu urged me, more than once, to call our adventure in Kathmandu 'Om Manipadmey Hoomicide'. When I told him that would be going a bit overboard, he said 'Hoommmm!', and sat twirling his prayer wheel, looking positively put out.